There's a Witch in My Dryer

To Finley,
Never stop believing...

Linda Lee Cross

Linda Lee Cross

2.9.2019

There's a Witch in My Dryer

iUniverse books may be ordered through booksellers or by contacting:

iUniverse
1663 Liberty Drive
Bloomington, IN 47403
www.iuniverse.com
1-800-Authors (1-800-288-4677)

Because of the dynamic nature of the internet, any web addresses or links contained in this book may have changed since publication and may no longer be valid. The views expressed in this work are solely those of the author and do not necessarily reflect the views of the publisher, and the publisher hereby disclaims any responsibility for them.

Any people depicted in stock imagery provided by Getty Images are models, and such images are being used for illustrative purposes only.
Certain stock imagery © Getty Images.

ISBN: 978-1-5320-5171-5 (hc)
ISBN: 978-1-5320-5172-2 (sc)
ISBN: 978-1-5320-5173-9 (e)

Library of Congress Control Number: 2018908792

Print information available on the last page.

iUniverse rev. date: 08/24/2018

This story is for my daughter,
Bre. She truly does believe!

Once there was a little girl who would sit very quietly on the laundry-room floor and watch her mother tend to the daily laundry. The dryer made a very unusual sound, and it seemed like her mother was always looking for some piece of clothing or another that was missing from the dryer. Her mother would always say, "It must have been misplaced. The dryer never loses anything."

One day the little girl was sitting on the floor next to the dryer and asked her mother, "What is that noise coming from the dryer?"

"Oh," her mother said, "that's the dryer's *clickety-clang-clickety-clack* sound. It's only pennies, nickels, and buckles making that noise."

Each morning her mother would tend to the laundry, and the little girl would listen even more closely than she had the day before. *Clickety-clang-clickety-clack* went the dryer.

"Hmmmm," said the little girl. "This does not sound like pennies, nickels, and buckles to me!"

The mother thought for a moment and then looked back at the little girl and said, "I seem to remember when I was a little girl just like you that I would ask your grandmother the same questions. Was it only a dream? Could it really be happening again? I think it is time for a visit from your grandmother."

The little girl was very excited to see her grandmother, and that evening they waited for her to arrive.

At exactly 6:30 p.m., her grandmother came through the door. She was carrying a large old bag, and inside was a very special gift for the little girl.

The grandmother asked the little girl's mother, "Do we have company?"

All of a sudden the mother looked up.

"So it was real! All those years ago?"

"Yes!" said the grandmother. "But once you started growing up, you stopped believing. As most grown-ups do.

"I have brought her the magic flashlight, which my mother gave to me and I then gave to you many years ago. This magic flashlight will only work for those who truly do believe."

The grandmother then opened her bag, reached all the way down to the bottom, and pulled out a very unusual flashlight. It was silver in color and looked very old. The little girl had never seen anything like it.

"What is this for?" said the little girl.

Her grandmother whispered in her ear, "This is a magic flashlight. Tonight, when all is quiet, take it down to the dryer. Turn it on, and all your questions will be answered."

That night the little girl could hardly wait to go to bed. When all was quiet, she crept out of her bedroom and went straight to the dryer. She turned on the flashlight and opened the dryer door. She pointed it way to the back, through the holes, and looked inside. But nothing was there.

"Hmmm," said the little girl, and she shut the dryer door.

As she began to walk away, she heard a noise.

"Excuse me? *Hello!*"

It was coming from the dryer. The little girl raced back to the dryer door and shined the flashlight way into the back. She could hardly believe her eyes. It was a witch, a real witch!

"Hi there," said the witch.

"H-h-hi," said the little girl,
almost afraid to answer.

"Well, I guess the secret's out," said the
witch, with a twinkle in her eye.

"Yeah!" said the little girl. "I knew it! I knew it all
the time. The *clickity-clang-clickity-clack* was you."

The witch began to explain. "A very long
time ago when your mother was a little girl
just like you, she also believed and found
me living in her dryer with the same magic
flashlight, but she grew up like all grown-
ups do and stopped believing in me."

"Sorry for all the noise," said the witch. "I get carried away in here sometimes, making my brews and getting ready for Halloween."

"Wow," said the little girl. "You really are a witch, and you live in my dryer!"

"Why, yes!" said the witch. "All of us witches live in dryers. Each little boy or girl who truly does believe will find a friendly witch living in their dryer."

"But you're not scary. You're a nice witch," said the little girl.

"Indeed!" said the witch. "We are all nice witches. We just do spooky things around Halloween to scare everyone. It's our job, you know."

The little girl and the witch became very good friends. After that night, whenever the little girl needed a friend, she would take her magic flashlight and open the dryer door, and the witch would be there.

One night the little girl came
down to visit the witch.

"Watcha doin'?" asked the little girl.

"Well, it is getting close to Halloween, so I'm
putting together my witch's costume."

"Oh," said the little girl. "I like your socks!
My mom has a pair just like that!"

They both began to laugh.

"I have found such treasures over the years that have fallen through the cracks of the dryer—pennies, nickels, buckles, and *socks*!" said the witch.

"Oh, yes!" said the little girl. "My mom always says, 'The dryer never loses anything.' I guess she was right all along."

The next morning, the little girl's mother was tending to the laundry as usual. She noticed that one red-and-white-striped sock was missing.

"Where in the world has this one sock gone?" asked her mother. "I put both of them into the dryer, but only one came out!"

The little girl giggled. "I'm sure it hasn't gone far. Remember, Mom, the dryer never loses anything!"

The End

CPSIA information can be obtained
at www.ICGtesting.com
Printed in the USA
LVHW071951070119
603021LV00025B/1476/P